P9-BYY-284

Mrs. Noodlekugel
and Drooly the Bear

Mrs. Noodlekugel
AND Drooly the Bear

Daniel Pinkwater
illustrated by
Adam Stower

CANDLEWICK PRESS

Text copyright © 2015 by Daniel Pinkwater
Illustrations copyright © 2015 by Adam Stower

First edition 2015

Library of Congress Catalog Card Number 2014945448
ISBN 978-0-7636-6645-3

15 16 17 18 19 20 BVG 10 9 8 7 6 5 4 3 2 1

Printed in Berryville, VA, U.S.A.

This book was typeset in Esprit.
The illustrations were done in ink.

Candlewick Press
99 Dover Street
Somerville, Massachusetts 02144

visit us at www.candlewick.com

For Jill, who else?
D. P.

For Jude and Anna
A. S.

Chapter
1

W e have to go away," Nick and
Maxine's mother said. "We are going to
the speed-knitting world championship
in Cleveland, Ohio. Your father is going
to compete."

"This is exciting," Nick and Maxine
said. "Our father has a chance to be

the speed-knitting champion of the world!"

"It is an honor just to be a finalist," their father said. "And here is a pair of socks for each of you. It took twenty-four minutes to do both pairs."

"They are beautiful socks," Nick and Maxine said. "Will we stay in a big hotel in Cleveland, Ohio?"

"Well, here is the thing," their mother said.

"Tell us the thing," Nick and Maxine said.

"The thing is, you are not coming with us."

"We are not?"

"No. Your father will be busy competing, and I have to be there to encourage him. There will be no one to look after you. We thought you could stay with Mrs. Noodlekugel. Would that be all right?"

Nick and Maxine looked at each other. They smiled. Mrs. Noodlekugel was their babysitter. She lived in a little house behind the big apartment building. Mrs. Noodlekugel was interesting. She had a cat named Mr.

Fuzzface. She had taught him to talk, and he had taught himself to play the piano. Also, Oldface, Mr. Fuzzface's father, lived with Mrs. Noodlekugel. He could talk, too, and there were four mice who wore glasses.

"Yes, we could stay with Mrs. Noodlekugel," Maxine said.

"Staying with Mrs. Noodlekugel would be all right," Nick said.

Nick and Maxine looked at each other and smiled again.

"We will only be gone four days," their mother said.

"It will be fine," Nick and Maxine said.

Nick and Maxine had been sent to stay with Mrs. Noodlekugel before for just a few hours, when their parents went shopping or went to the wrestling matches. Sometimes they had stayed with Mrs. Noodlekugel for a whole day, but they had never slept over, and they had never stayed for four whole days.

Chapter 2

Mrs. Noodlekugel's house was hidden behind the big apartment building where Nick and Maxine lived. To get there, Nick and Maxine had to take the elevator down to the basement. They had to go past the little room where Mike the janitor sat, listening to the radio, eating stewed tomatoes out of a can, and talking to himself. Then they had to go through the boiler room, full of pipes and machinery, and through a little door. Then they were in a backyard, with grass and dandelions, and in the middle was the little house and the little garden.

On the porch of the little house, enjoying the sunshine, were two cats, Fuzzface and Oldface.

"Nick and Maxine are here," Fuzz-face called out.

"Dese kids is here!" Oldface, who was Fuzzface's father, called out.

"Tell them to come right in," Nick and Maxine heard Mrs. Noodlekugel call from inside the house.

Carrying two beautiful knitted suitcases their father had made, Nick and Maxine went into the house.

Mrs. Noodlekugel was wearing her apron. "I am just cutting up vegetables," Mrs. Noodlekugel said. "After you put your beautiful suitcases away, perhaps you would like to help?"

13

"Where should we put our suit-cases?" Nick and Maxine asked.

"Just go up the stairs to the top of the house. You will share a room with the mice. I hope you will not mind."

There were four mice who lived in Mrs. Noodlekugel's house. The mice all wore glasses, and they were very nice mice.

"We will not mind sharing a room with the mice," Nick said.

"We like the mice," Maxine said.

"At bedtime, perhaps you would help the mice put on their nightshirts," Mrs. Noodlekugel asked.

"Why do the mice wear nightshirts to sleep in when they don't wear anything during the day?"

"Oh, one must have nightclothes," Mrs. Noodlekugel said.

"We brought pajamas," Nick and Maxine said.

"Pajamas are fine, but the mice prefer nightshirts," Mrs. Noodlekugel said.

Chapter 3

When Nick and Maxine came down-stairs after putting their suitcases away, Mrs. Noodlekugel said, "Would you like to help Mr. Fuzzface set the table? We are having cake for supper."

"Cake for supper? At our house, we sometimes have cake for dessert."

"For dessert, we are having soup."

"Cake for supper, and soup for dessert?" Nick asked.

"The sweet thing first, and the soup thing after?" Maxine asked.

"It is not a sweet cake," Mrs. Noodlekugel said. "It is a vegetable cake. It has mushrooms. And the soup is a sweet soup. It has chocolate drops."

"Why there isn't sardines?" Oldface said. "Should be there is sardines. Sardines in cake, and sardines in soup."

"Mr. Oldface, you would have sardines in everything," Mrs. Noodlekugel said.

"Yes! You is right, lady," Oldface said. "Sardines is good."

"Father dear, do not put your feet on the table," Fuzzface said. "It is bad manners."

"Such a fancy fellow," Oldface said.

"Please call the mice," Mrs. Noodlekugel said.

"Mices! Come eat!" Oldface called. "Is cake without sardines."

The four mice, wearing their eyeglasses, scurried into the room and climbed up the tablecloth.

"How come mices get to put feet on table?" Oldface asked.

"They are mice," Fuzzface said. "It is different."

Mrs. Noodlekugel tore a paper napkin into four squares, and the mice tucked them under their chins. The mice got crumbs of vegetable cake all over themselves and all over the tablecloth. When dessert was served, they got chocolate-drop soup on their eyeglasses.

It was good cake and good soup. Nick and Maxine found it interesting to watch Fuzzface and Oldface eat with forks and spoons.

Chapter 4

Maxine and Nick helped Fuzzface clear the table. Then Mrs. Noodlekugel got out her knitting, and Fuzzface played the piano and sang. He played the only song he knew, "Three Blind Mice," but he sang it as "Four Blind Mice."

"Fuzzface plays nice," Oldface said. "He talks nice. Mrs. Noodlekugel lady taught him talk nice — not like his fadder, not like Oldface. Oldface was taught talk by rough sailormen."

"Mr. Oldface was an offshore kitty," Mrs. Noodlekugel said.

"Oldface used to sail the seven seas," Oldface said. "Like Captain Noodlekugel."

"Captain Noodlekugel?" Nick and Maxine asked.

"Mrs. Noodlekugel's mister," Oldface said. "This is him, in painting."

On the wall was a large painting of an old-fashioned sailing ship in a terrible storm. On the deck stood a man with wonderful whiskers.

"That is Captain Noodlekugel?" Nick asked.

"Lost at sea," Mrs. Noodlekugel said.

LOST at SEA

"He was drowned?" Maxine asked.

"No, just lost," Mrs. Noodlekugel said. "He is often lost. Sometimes he finds his way home; sometimes he sends a letter. He is usually lost."

The mice began to yawn.

Chapter 5

Nick and Maxine led the mice upstairs. The mice had little bunk beds, four of them, stacked one on top of another. The bunk beds were on top of a chest of drawers.

It was a hard job getting the mice into their nightshirts. The mice wriggled and squirmed, and when Nick and Maxine had gotten one mouse into his nightshirt, another had wiggled out of his.

"We should get one mouse into a nightshirt and then tuck him into bed," Maxine said. "Then we can work together. We'll do one mouse at a time."

"They keep wriggling," Nick said. "Look — this one has put both paws and a foot into the sleeve. These are terrible mice."

One by one, the brother and sister got the mice into nightshirts and tucked into their bunk beds. They folded the mice's eyeglasses and put them under their pillows.

It was not over. The mice giggled and squeaked and kicked the covers loose.

"Tuck them in tight," Maxine said. "You are terrible mice!" This made the mice giggle and squeak even more.

"I'll bet Mr. Oldface knows how to handle these mice," Nick said. "I am going to call him."

The mice instantly stopped squeaking and thrashing.

"I think we found the secret," Maxine whispered.

Soon the mice were snoring tiny mouselike snores.

"That was a lot of work," Nick said. "I am ready to tuck myself into my own little bed."

"So am I," Maxine said.

And soon the children were snoring tiny mouselike snores themselves.

Chapter 6

When Nick and Maxine came downstairs in the morning, they found a little man with wonderful whiskers. The little man was dripping wet and had made puddles on the carpet.

"Are you Captain Noodlekugel?" Maxine asked.

"I am he. I am just back from the sea."

Mrs. Noodlekugel came in with a tray. "Here are cornflakes and sardines," she said.

"Sardines?" the children heard Oldface call from another room. "I will be right there."

"That is Mr. Oldface," Mrs. Noodlekugel said. "You have not met Mr. Oldface. He is Mr. Fuzzface's father."

"I am his fadder," Oldface said. "Where are sardines?"

"He is my father," Fuzzface said. "I would like some sardines, too."

"And these are Nick and Maxine," Mrs. Noodlekugel said. "They are staying for a few days."

"I am pleased to meet you all." Captain Noodlekugel bowed, dripping.

"Were you lost at sea?" Nick asked.

"I have given up the sea," Captain Noodlekugel said. "I will do something else."

"Perhaps that is a good idea," Mrs. Noodlekugel said. "The sea is so . . . damp."

"Do we have to put sardines on our cornflakes?" Maxine asked.

"No, dear," Mrs. Noodlekugel said. "Only the Captain and the cats like them that way."

"Captain Noodlekugel is real sailorman," Oldface said.

"What will you do, now that you have given up the sea?" Nick asked.

"I will be an animal trainer," Captain Noodlekugel said. "I will join a circus."

"Lions and tigers?" Maxine asked.

"Maybe," Captain Noodlekugel said. "First I have to practice. I will begin with a bear."

"Are bears easier to train?" Fuzzface asked.

"Where will you find a bear?" Mrs. Noodlekugel asked.

"I have already found a bear," Captain Noodlekugel said. "I brought him with me."

Everyone looked around. "Where is the bear?"

"He is outside in the garden. His name is Drooly. Would you all like to see Drooly?"

Chapter
7

Everyone followed Captain Noodlekugel outside, except the mice. The mice had run upstairs when Captain Noodlekugel said he had brought a bear.

"Drooly is around here somewhere. Ah! There he is!"

There was a bear taking a nap in Mrs. Noodlekugel's garden. It was a large bear.

"He is squashing my petunias!" Mrs. Noodlekugel said.

"We see why you call him Drooly," Nick and Maxine said.

"He does drool a bit," Captain Noodlekugel said. "Wake up, Drooly! Say hello to the people and the cats!"

Drooly opened one eye. Then he opened the other eye. Then he closed both eyes. He went back to sleep.

"Up, Drooly! Up, sir!" Captain Noodlekugel snapped an imaginary whip. Drooly sat up slowly.

"Ask him to get off my petunias," Mrs. Noodlekugel said.

"This is Drooly," Captain Noodlekugel said. "Drooly, stand up!"

Drooly got to his feet slowly.

"Drooly, bow to the people!"

Drooly scratched himself.

"I have just begun to train him," Captain Noodlekugel said.

"Would Drooly like some breakfast?" Mrs. Noodlekugel asked. "Does Drooly like cornflakes?"

"I am sure Drooly would love to have cornflakes," Captain Noodlekugel said.

"Mr. Fuzzface, would you bring a bowl of cornflakes for the bear?" Mrs. Noodlekugel asked.

"A large bowl," Captain Noodlekugel said.

Drooly will have his cornflakes on the porch while we finish our breakfast," Captain Noodlekugel said. "He is a bit large to sit at the table."

"And there is the drooling," Mrs. Noodlekugel said.

"Yes, there is that."

"Also, Drooly has a bit of an odor."

"I plan to give him a bath."

"Drooly is not dangerous, is he?"

"Oh, no. Drooly is a good-natured bear. The man I bought him from said he is as tame as a kitten," Captain Noodlekugel said.

"Ha!" Oldface said.

"And you think Drooly can be a bear in a circus?" Nick asked.

"Not now. Not as he is now. I have to teach him tricks, and how to dance, and how to ride a bicycle. Just imagine! Drooly will be bathed, and I will brush his fur. Maybe he will wear a little hat. Won't that be splendid? On a bicycle?"

"How did you happen to buy Drooly?" Maxine asked.

"It is interesting," Captain Noodle-kugel said. "I was shipwrecked at the time . . ."

"The Captain is often ship-wrecked," Mrs. Noodlekugel said.

"I was shipwrecked, and floating along. I had climbed up onto a piece of wood, and was perfectly comfortable, when this Inuit fellow came along in a canoe. With him, he had a bear.

"'Are you in any difficulty?' the Inuit fellow asked me.

"'No, merely shipwrecked,' I said. 'That is a nice bear you have.'

"'You like him?' the Inuit fellow asked.

"'Well, I don't pretend to be an expert on bears,' I said.

"'Oh?'

"'But he seems a very fine bear to me.'

"'He is the best bear I ever owned,' the Inuit fellow said. 'But keeping him is a problem. He fights with my husky

sled dogs. And I am a poor man—
feeding him costs a lot.'

"'Would you consider selling him?'

"'I don't know.'

"'I can offer you this Mexican
dollar, my gold watch, a fish I caught a
little while ago, and this piece of wood
I am floating on, for the bear and your
canoe.'

"'Sir,' the Inuit fellow said, 'although we have only just met, out here in the middle of the ocean, I have taken a great liking to you. I know you are a fine man, and will take good care of my bear.'

"And so, the Inuit chap floated away on my piece of wood, singing a little song, and Drooly and I paddled off in the canoe."

"How did you find your way back from the middle of the ocean?" Nick asked.

Captain Noodlekugel began to speak, but he was interrupted.

"What was that noise?" Mrs. Noodlekugel asked. "Mr. Fuzzface, please go see what made that noise."

Fuzzface went out, then came back. "The bear has broken the porch," he said.

"Broken the porch?"

"Only part of the porch. Now he is sleeping again. I will repair it later."

"You must remember, Drooly is in a strange place," Captain Noodlekugel said. "It will take him a little while to get used to things."

"Of course," Mrs. Noodlekugel said.

Chapter 9

For the rest of the morning, Captain Noodlekugel trained Drooly in the garden. Mrs. Noodlekugel, Nick and Maxine, Oldface, and Fuzzface sat on the unbroken part of the porch and watched. The mice watched from an upstairs window.

The training went slowly. At first, Drooly did not understand what Captain Noodlekugel wanted him to do. Then he forgot what he had learned. Also, he fell asleep very often. And he squashed many plants and flowers.

Captain Noodlekugel showed Drooly how to balance on one foot. Drooly balanced, wobbled, and sat down on a bed of pansies.

Then he tried to balance on a big ball, and fell flat on some daisies.

"We will try a somersault," Captain Noodlekugel said.

Mrs. Noodlekugel held her breath.

The bear took out some lilies, ferns, and roses.

"We will have to do the entire garden over," Mrs. Noodlekugel said to Fuzzface.

"I was thinking the same thing," Fuzzface said.

Drooly had fallen asleep on top of Mrs. Noodlekugel's tulips.

"I am going to prepare lunch," Mrs. Noodlekugel said. "Captain, will the bear eat toasted cheese sandwiches?"

"They are his favorite," Captain Noodlekugel said.

Chapter 10

Lunch was nearly over. Captain and Mrs. Noodlekugel and Nick and Maxine had finished the toasted cheese sandwiches and were nibbling pickles. Fuzzface was beginning to clear the table. The mice had come down and eaten some crumbs.

Oldface came in. "Bear is gone," he said.

"Gone? What do you mean, gone?"

"Gone. Went. Not here anymore."

"How could he be gone? Where did he go?"

"Broke fence. Don't know where went," Oldface said. "Looks like wandered off."

"Well, bears do wander," Captain Noodlekugel said. "He may just wander back."

"Do you think he will wander back?"

"No. Usually they just wander and wander. We will have to look for him."

Everyone went out in the garden. The fence was broken, and Drooly was gone.

"We will track him," Captain Noodlekugel said.

"Maybe he left a trail of drool," Nick said.

"That is disgusting," Maxine said.

"He does not drool that much," Captain Noodlekugel said. "We should look for things he has squashed with his feet."

"Later we will repair the fence," Mrs. Noodlekugel told Fuzzface.

"Look in the trees. Sometimes bears climb trees," Captain Noodlekugel said.

"We do not see him in any trees," Nick and Maxine said.

"Look for hollow logs," Captain Noodlekugel said. "Bears like to hide in hollow logs."

"There are no hollow logs," Nick and Maxine said.

"You know, there are tall apartment buildings all around us," Fuzzface said. "There are no spaces between the buildings for him to wander through."

"Then he is hiding nearby!" Captain Noodlekugel said. "Drooly! Where are you, Drooly? Come, Drooly! Nice Drooly!"

Captain Noodlekugel, Mrs. Noodle-kugel, Nick, Maxine, Fuzzface, and Oldface walked in all directions, whistling and calling. "Drooly! Drooly! Where are you, Drooly?"

Chapter
11

How can something as big as a bear hide in an area this small?" Captain Noodlekugel asked.

"Is not hide," Oldface said. "Is gone."

"How can he be gone? There are buildings all around."

"Gone out same way you came in," Oldface said. "How you came in?"

"Let me think," Captain Noodlekugel said. "How did I come in? That is a good question. How did I come in?"

"The Captain has a poor sense of direction," Mrs. Noodlekugel said. "That is why he gets lost at sea."

"*We* came in through our apartment building," Nick and Maxine said.

"Of course you did!" Captain Noodlekugel said. "Clever children! Show us how you did it!"

Nick and Maxine showed Captain Noodlekugel the little door in their apartment building, and everyone crowded through.

Chapter 12

They found Drooly sitting in the little room with Mike the janitor. They were eating stewed tomatoes out of cans and listening to the radio.

"Is this your bear?" Mike the Janitor asked. "He is a nice bear."

"Thank you for looking after my bear," Captain Noodlekugel said.

"You will sleep in the garden tonight," Captain Noodlekugel told Drooly. "Mrs. Noodlekugel will lend you some blankets. Do not wander away. In the morning we will go somewhere. I have a new plan."

"What is your new plan?" Mrs. Noodlekugel asked.

"I have decided to go back to sea. I will take Drooly with me. He will make a fine able-bodied sea bear."

"Yes, that is a good plan."

That night Nick and Maxine struggled with the mice, trying to tuck them in.

"It is interesting staying with Mrs. Noodlekugel," Maxine said.

"Yes, it is," Nick said. "I wonder what will happen tomorrow."